L 6.8
lpt.
290

C
H
I
C
A
G
O

RICHARD RAMBECK

THE HISTORY OF THE
WHITE SOX

CREATIVE EDUCATION

Published by Creative Education
123 South Broad Street, Mankato, Minnesota 56001
Creative Education is an imprint of The Creative Company

Designed by Rita Marshall
Editorial assistance by Julie Bach and John Nichols

Photos by: Allsport Photography, Corbis-Bettmann, Focus on Sports, Fotosport, SportsChrome.

Library of Congress Cataloging-in-Publication Data

Rambeck, Richard.
The History of the Chicago White Sox / by Richard Rambeck.
p. cm. — (Baseball)
Summary: Highlights the key personalities and memorable games in the history of the team that was founded by Charles Comiskey in 1901.
ISBN: 0-88682-904-6

1. Chicago White Sox (Baseball team)—History—Juvenile literature.
[1. Chicago White Sox (Baseball team)—History. 2. Baseball—History.]
I. Title. II. Series: Baseball (Mankato, Minn.)

GV875.C58R355   1999
796.357'64'0977311—dc21   97-7131

9 8 7 6 5 4 3 2

With the exception of New York City, no U.S. city has played a larger role in this country's economy than Chicago. Situated on the southern tip of Lake Michigan in the northern part of Illinois, Chicago is a major water port as well as a hub of railroad and airplane transportation. Its location makes it an ideal center for trade and cultural activities for the Midwestern United States. The winds that blow off Lake Michigan straight through Chicago's downtown fit the community's nickname of the "Windy City."

In one century, from 1850 to 1950, the metropolis, also known as the "Second City," grew from a town of a little

Chicago greats Eddie Cicotte (left) and Clarence Rowland.

On April 24, the first official AL game was played in Chicago, and Ray Patterson defeated Cleveland 8–2.

more than 29,000 people to a huge urban area with more than 3.6 million residents. Chicago was the second-largest city in the United States up until the late 1980s, but it is now third behind New York and Los Angeles. Chicago's O'Hare International Airport is the busiest in the United States, handling more than 60 million airline passengers a year.

The city has a rich history, including a love for our national pastime—baseball. Chicagoans have flocked to ballparks for more than 100 years to watch professional baseball. The city has been able to support not one but two major-league teams throughout the 20th century. This is the story of Chicago's American League franchise, the White Sox, a team based in the city's South Side.

The White Sox were among the charter members of the American League, which commenced play in 1901. That first year it was one of the top clubs in the league. Led by manager Clark Griffith and star player Fielder Jones, the White Sox won the first American League pennant with an 83–53 record. No World Series was played that year; the American and National league champions did not start meeting in postseason competition until 1903.

Five years after the beginning of the American League, Chicago was the site of the first intra-city World Series, which featured the National League champion Chicago Cubs and the American League pennant-winning White Sox. The South Siders won the battle of Chicago four games to two behind the pitching of Frank "Yip" Owens, Nick Altrock, and Guy "Doc" White. White Sox owner Charles Comiskey was so thrilled with his team's performance that he awarded the players and coaches $15,000 in bonuses.

Multitalented second baseman Ray Durham.

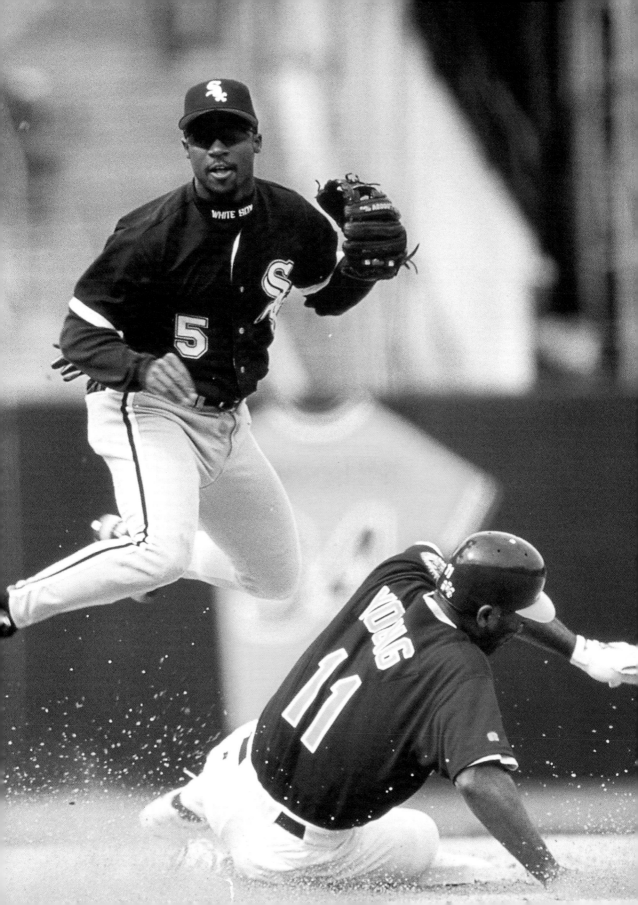

1 9 1 5

The Chicago club purchased the contract of "Shoeless" Joe Jackson from Cleveland for a sum of $31,500.

After winning the 1906 World Series, the White Sox couldn't maintain their top position. They became a middle-of-the-pack club in the eight-team American League and remained one until 1915, when a new manager and a new star joined the team. The manager was Clarence "Pants" Rowland. The star was a country boy from South Carolina named Joe Jackson. People called him "Shoeless" because of his poverty-stricken upbringing.

Jackson had played previously for the Philadelphia Athletics and the Cleveland Indians. He was an outstanding fielder—but an even better hitter. No less than superstar Ty Cobb of the Detroit Tigers called Jackson "the finest natural hitter in the history of the game." A young slugger with the Boston Red Sox named Babe Ruth tried to imitate Jackson's swing. "I copied Jackson's hitting style because I thought he was the greatest hitter I'd ever seen," Ruth explained years later. "I still think the same way." Perhaps the biggest compliment directed toward Jackson came from Washington Senators star pitcher Walter Johnson, a man never known to praise anyone. "I consider Joe Jackson the greatest natural ballplayer I've ever seen," he said.

Led by Jackson, outfielder Oscar "Happy" Felsch, and pitchers Eddie Cicotte and Urban "Red" Faber, the White Sox rolled up 100 victories in 1917 to win the American League pennant. In the World Series against the powerful New York Giants, the White Sox claimed their second major-league championship by winning the series four games to two. Faber won two games and saved a third.

Two years later, the mighty Sox were in the World Series again due to pitchers Eddie Cicotte, who won 29 games and lost only seven, and Claude "Lefty" Williams, who won 23 games. But during the series, Cicotte and Williams were ineffective. Together they lost five games to the Cincinnati Reds, who won the best-of-nine series five to three.

In his first year as manager, Kid Gleason led the Sox to an 88–52 record and the AL pennant.

One year after the White Sox lost the Series to the Reds, Cicotte made a surprising confession. He admitted to accepting a $10,000 bribe from gamblers to throw the World Series. Baseball fans were shocked as more of the story unfolded. Supposedly, gamblers had paid first baseman Charles "Chick" Gandil, who then allegedly passed the money on to other Chicago players, including Williams, Felsch, Swede Risberg, Fred McMullin, Buck Weaver, and Jackson.

The eight players, who became known as the "Black Sox," went to trial and were acquitted on all charges. But baseball commissioner Kenesaw Mountain Landis was not convinced that the Black Sox were innocent. He banned them all from baseball for life.

Jackson, who finished his major-league career with a .356 batting average, third on the all-time list, never stopped fighting to clear his name. The star slugger, who could neither read nor write, admitted that he took $5,000 from Gandil, but then thought about giving the money back. He wanted to turn the money over to Comiskey, but he decided against it. If Jackson had tried to fix the series, he went about it in a strange way. During the series, he batted .375, committed no errors, and compiled 12 hits, a World Series record that stood until 1964.

Forty years after Jackson's death, some fans are still trying

Powerful pitcher Eric King.

Fleet-footed Sammy Sosa. 11

1 9 5 1

Minnie Minoso, making his White Sox debut, became the first black player on the team.

to clear his name and get him inducted into baseball's Hall of Fame. "Joe Jackson has been out of baseball 70 years," wrote Donald Gropman in his biography of Jackson titled *Say It Ain't So, Joe!* "Why does he keep popping up? He's a metaphor for something—the Huckleberry Finn of baseball. He had that naive innocence and was chewed up and spit out. And his ghost has never been quite laid to rest." Jackson, who later learned to read and write and eventually became a successful businessman, went to his grave in 1951 maintaining his innocence. On his deathbed he looked up at his wife and said, "I'm going to meet the greatest umpire of all—and he knows I'm innocent."

"GO GO" SOX BREAK LOSING SPELL

After losing such stars as Joe Jackson, Eddie Cicotte, Lefty Williams, and Buck Weaver, the White Sox fell into a terrible slump, one that would endure through an almost endless succession of losing seasons. There were few highlights during this awful stretch, except for Luke Appling's two batting titles in 1936 and 1943. The club went through a series of managers: Ed Collins, Ray Schalk, Donie Bush, Lew Fonseca, Ted Lyons, and Jack Onslow. Finally, Paul Richards took the helm and began to turn things around. The White Sox led the American League for 44 days in 1951 before winding up in fourth place. The 1957 team ended the season in second place, the club's highest finish in 37 years.

Chicago White Sox fans finally had a team with a positive identity—the club was known as the "Go Go White Sox" because of its tremendous speed and base-stealing ability.

Shortstop Luis Aparicio led the American League in steals from 1956 to 1959. Second baseman Nellie Fox was one of the finest natural hitters in the game. Together they formed an awesome double-play combination. Center fielder Jim Landis and first baseman Earl Torgeson hit with power, and pitcher Bill Pierce blazed his fastball past opposing hitters. Knuckleball pitcher Hoyt Wilhelm mystified batters with his fluttering pitch.

Future Hall-of-Famer Nellie Fox led the "Go Go Sox" with a .306 batting average.

The White Sox had become the most entertaining thing to hit the South Side in years, and new owner Bill Veeck was determined to win the fans over with a show-biz approach. He built a scoreboard in Chicago's Comiskey Park that shot off fireworks, and he played music when the White Sox made a good play. Veeck amused the fans before games with bareback riders, elephants, sword-swallowers, and clowns.

But the players were the most exciting performers on the program in 1959. They were led by manager Al Lopez, pitcher Early Wynn, who won 22 games and the American League Cy Young Award, and Fox, the league's Most Valuable Player. The White Sox rolled to a 94–60 record and their first American League pennant in 40 years. In the first game of the World Series, Chicago surprised the National League champion Los Angeles Dodgers with an 11–0 victory. Unfortunately, the Dodgers rebounded to take four of the next five games and won the series four games to two. Chicago's best season in four decades had ended. South Side fans would wait 24 years before they could cheer another championship team.

1 9 7 1

Bill Melton not only led the league in homers (33), but played fine defense for Chicago.

During the 1960s, Chicago might have been the best team in baseball that did not win a pennant. The White Sox finished second in the American League three straight years, from 1963 through 1965. In 1967, they went into the final week of the season with an excellent chance to finish first, but then faded and lost out to the Boston Red Sox. It would be another decade before Chicago would again contend for a pennant.

Even though the team stumbled a bit during the 1970s, several players contributed outstanding individual performances. Hard-hitting third baseman Bill Melton led the American League in home runs in 1971 with 33. The following season Dick Allen, Chicago's star first baseman, topped the league in homers (37) and runs batted in (113) and was named the league's Most Valuable Player. Allen also won the American League home-run title in 1974 with 32 home runs. "Those two [Allen and Melton] are murder," griped Oakland A's manager Dick Williams. "Our guys just hate facing them."

Despite the heroics of their two sluggers, the White Sox lagged behind the contenders in the American League West Division during the 1970s. (In 1969, the American League had been split into two divisions, the East and the West.) But the team's fortunes started to change when Tony La Russa was named manager of the club in 1979. The White Sox began to improve, and when veteran catcher Carlton "Pudge" Fisk signed on as a free agent, it was time to start winning again.

14

Hard-throwing LaMarr Hoyt.

Strong-armed Melido Perez.

Led by manager Tony La Russa and the strong hitting of Chet Lemon and Lamar Johnson, the White Sox raced to the lead in the AL West in the early part of the 1980 season. By the end of the season, however, the Sox faded to fifth place. It was a bitter disappointment to owner Bill Veeck, who then sold the team to real estate baron Jerry Reinsdorf and lawyer Eddie Einhorn. The new owners moved quickly and boldly by signing free-agent catcher Carlton "Pudge" Fisk to a five-year, $2.9 million contract. Fisk had spent nine years with the Boston Red Sox and was 33 years old—almost ancient by catching standards. But Fisk knew how to take care of himself. He maintained a strenuous exercise program that many teammates thought was too taxing. Fisk, however, believed that keeping fit was essential.

First baseman Mike Squiers captured the Gold Glove award for his fielding excellence during the season.

"Success has no shortcut, only a high price of pain and humiliation," he explained. "I may seem like some crusty old New Englander, but if you're going to do something, do it right, or don't do it at all." Of his exercise program, Fisk said, "This work has strengthened my legs so that it's actually easier for me to catch today than it was 10 years ago. I think this physical commitment has maintained my focus and ability to concentrate. Baseball requires mental strength. The season has a lot of 'give-in' days. The commitment overcomes that."

Fisk showed his commitment to winning by having a breakout year in 1983. He hit 26 home runs, drove in 86 runs, and batted .330 during the season's last four months. He also expertly handled a pitching staff that included

The steady Carlton Fisk (pages 18-19).

American League Cy Young Award winner LaMarr Hoyt. The pitchers received offensive help from outfielder Ron Kittle, whose 35 homers and 100 RBIs earned him the American League Rookie of the Year title. In addition, designated hitter Greg Luzinski chipped in 32 homers.

Ron Kittle bashed 35 homers and drove in 100 runs, earning him the AL Rookie of the Year award.

As a result of these performances, the White Sox, who lost 24 of their first 40 games, rebounded to win the AL West by an astounding 20 games over second-place Kansas City. It was the largest margin of victory in an American League race in nearly 50 years. La Russa, the architect of the team's success, was named the 1983 Manager of the Year.

But La Russa and the White Sox saw their luck run out in the American League Championship Series against Baltimore. The Orioles lost the first game of the best-of-five series, but then rallied for three straight victories to claim the pennant. The White Sox vowed to return to postseason play the following year, but it was not to be. The team went from AL West champs in 1983 to chumps in 1984, posting a 74–88 record, a 25-game slide from the previous season. "I'm just happy the season is over," said a dejected La Russa. Most of the Chicago stars slumped in 1984, but there was one exception: right fielder Harold Baines.

QUIET BAINES LETS HIS BAT DO THE TALKING

Unlike most stars, Baines wasn't flashy. He didn't talk much, and if it weren't for the fact that he almost always seemed to be playing well, most fans probably wouldn't have noticed him. "He does his job diligently and smoothly, with little fanfare," said White Sox general manager Roland Hemond. "His personality shows up in game-winning situations. People who've been jumping up and down all day have nothing left. Harold's ready." Baines proved his value in clutch situations during the 1983 season, when he set a major-league record with 22 game-winning RBIs. Even Baines' sworn enemies—opposing pitchers—expressed grudging respect for his ability to adjust at the plate. "He has excellent hand-eye coordination," explained Texas Rangers pitcher Frank Tanana. "He'll pick up the pitch right away, tell what kind it is and how fast it's going, and then pop it." Baines believed his batting success was based on studying the opposition. "I'm a guess hitter," he said. "I guess with the catcher because he calls the game. Before I bat, I'll watch how the catcher works a hitter they might pitch the same as me. I try not to over-swing, and I concentrate harder after the seventh inning."

1 9 8 4

Tom Seaver went 15–11 to lead the White Sox in victories for the season.

Unfortunately for Baines and the White Sox during the 1984 season, few of his teammates had such an ability to concentrate in the late innings. The team lost 32 games by one run. The White Sox, who led the division at the All-Star break, faded into oblivion after that. Team management was disappointed enough to make major changes, one of which was to trade pitching ace LaMarr Hoyt to the San Diego Padres for several young players, including a shortstop named Ozzie Guillen.

GUILLEN TAKES THE SHORT ROUTE TO STARDOM

Ozzie Guillen was a natural acquisition for the White Sox, a team with a tradition of fine Latin American

The extraordinary Ron Kittle.

shortstops. Like Luis Aparicio, the team's great shortstop of the late 1950s and early 1960s, Guillen was born in Venezuela. Although only a rookie, he had the instincts of a veteran in the field. "Ozzie reminds me of Red Schoendienst when he came over to Milwaukee and solidified the defense in 1957," recalled White Sox general manager Roland Hemond, who played with Schoendienst in Milwaukee. "We'd say, 'What a great fielder, what instinct, what knowledge of the hitters.' But Red was 34; Ozzie's 21."

Opponents also marveled at Guillen's abilities in the field. Kansas City veteran second baseman Frank White claimed Guillen "has all the tools." Guillen worked on his "tools" by practicing his fielding as often as possible with a tiny mitt. "All the great Venezuelan shortstops use the same style as I do in fielding practice," he explained. "They take a small glove and try to catch everything one-handed. That makes your hand strong."

Guillen was also willing to work on other aspects of his game. In one game in 1985, he drew a walk and then threw his bat in the air, nearly hitting himself on the head. When Guillen reached first base, coach Joe Nossek said, "We better practice that, Ozzie, so you don't hurt yourself. Be out here early tomorrow." Nossek was kidding, but Guillen turned to him and said, "What time?"

Guillen's all-around play earned him the American League Rookie of the Year award in 1985. There were no team honors for the White Sox, however, as Chicago could not regain its 1983 form. In fact, the team slumped all the way to last place in 1989, posting the second-worst record in the American League. But out of the ashes of that awful

1 9 8 5

Hard-throwing Floyd Bannister averaged 8.46 strikeouts per nine innings— tops in the AL.

season emerged a new power in 1990. Most experts picked the White Sox to finish last in the seven-team American League West, but Chicago and manager Jeff Torborg had other ideas.

Guillen became one of the top hitters in the league. Outfielders Ivan Calderon, Sammy Sosa, and Lance Johnson all hit for power and average. Catcher Carlton Fisk had one of the top batting averages on the team, but his most important contribution to the White Sox was handling the club's superb young pitching staff. Starters Eric King, Melido Perez, and Greg Hibbard, all of whom were in their mid-20s, pitched extremely well in 1990. But their performances were almost second-rate compared to the contributions of Chicago's relief pitchers. Fireballing closer Bobby Thigpen

1 9 8 9

Carlton Fisk ripped his 2,000th career hit against the New York Yankees at Comiskey Park.

A reliable lead-off man, Lance Johnson.

slammed the door shut on opponents, setting a major-league record for saves in a season with 57. Barry Jones and Scott Radinsky helped out as well, combining for a 15–1 record during the first half of the 1990 season.

Largely due to a pitching staff that had one of the best earned-run averages in the major leagues, the White Sox went from losers in 1989 to contenders in 1990. They battled tooth-and-nail with the world champion Oakland A's for the American League West title before being edged out in the end. Experts said all year that the team's performance was a fluke, but the scrappy White Sox stuck with it and proved the experts wrong.

The club's exciting performance in 1990 made the last year of baseball in old Comiskey Park a memorable one. The ballpark, built in 1910, had been replaced with the new Comiskey Park right across the street. On September 30, 1990, the team played its final game at old Comiskey. The fans were elated to see the White Sox beat Seattle 2–1. The final regular-season record at old Comiskey reached 3,024 wins and 2,926 losses.

Closer Bobby Thig-pen set the major-league record for saves in a season with a total of 57.

"BIG HURT" BRUISES THE OPPOSITION

On April 18 the following spring, the White Sox played their first game in the new ballpark before a sellout crowd. They weren't as lucky as they had been the previous fall, however. The Detroit Tigers beat them 16–0. But along with a new ballpark, the White Sox fans were also treated to a new hero. A 6-foot-5 and 260-pound hulk of a first baseman by the name of Frank Thomas was beginning

Four-time Gold Glove winner Robin Ventura (pages 26-27).

Jack McDowell hurled four shutouts among his 22 victories, leading the league in both categories.

his first full season with the team. The former Auburn University football player's booming bat caused so much discomfort to baseballs that he quickly became known everywhere as the "Big Hurt." Thomas's rare combination of enormous power and sharp batting eye instantly made him one of the most feared hitters in the game. "I don't know where they found this kid," muttered Detroit Tigers pitcher Jack Morris. "But it's not fair for a guy to be that strong and yet still so disciplined at the plate. I have no idea how to get him out."

Thomas exploded on the scene in 1991, belting 32 homers and driving in 109 runs while finishing ninth in the league in hitting with a .318 mark. The White Sox, buoyed by their young slugger's performance, improved to 87–75 in 1991. "We've got a big horse now; it's time to ride him," said Guillen. By the end of the 1993 campaign, the Big Hurt had carried the White Sox all the way to the top of the American League West. His 41 homers, 128 RBIs, and .317 average fueled the team's high-octane offense, which also featured Fisk, third baseman Robin Ventura, and DH/outfielder Bo Jackson. The amazing Jackson had made a successful return to baseball after having surgery to replace a hip he had injured playing professional football for the Los Angeles Raiders. "Bo's so strong mentally and physically, it's an inspiration," noted Ventura.

After wrapping up the AL West, Jackson, Thomas, and the White Sox had to face the powerful Toronto Blue Jays in the American League Championship Series. The Sox battled fiercely, capturing games three and four, but eventually lost the series in six games. In 1994, the team resolved to return to the playoffs and bring a World Series title home, but they never got a chance. A players' strike ended the season prematurely, wasting a brilliant 67–46 start.

"I'll always wonder how that season [1994] would have ended," said Thomas, who won his second consecutive American League MVP award that year. "The strike hurt us, and it took a long time for us to get over it."

The Sox were shaken in 1995, and despite Thomas's 40 homers, 111 RBIs, and .308 average, the team sank to a 68–76 mark. The Sox began to recover in 1996, posting an 85–77 record, but owner Jerry Reinsdorf was growing impatient. He wanted the White Sox to duplicate the success of another Chicago pro team, basketball's Chicago Bulls, who had won the world championship several times during the '90s. Reinsdorf's fascination with the Bulls came naturally, as he owned both franchises. "I think the formula for winning is simple," he said. "With the Bulls, we put together the best players in the world, and we won. That's also my plan for the White Sox. It's that simple."

After the 1996 season, Reinsdorf put his plan into motion. The White Sox obtained free agent slugger Albert Belle from their American League Central rival the Cleveland Indians and also lured workhorse pitcher Jaime Navarro away from the crosstown Cubs. "With Belle and Ventura batting behind Frank, we're going to have an offense no one in baseball can match," said manager Terry Bevington. "And with Jaime as our ace, I like our chances." Unfortunately for Bevington, 1997 turned out to be a bitter disappointment. Ventura broke his ankle in spring training, and both Thomas and Belle got off to slow starts. Navarro was inconsistent,

Jason Bere notched another top single-game strikeout performance, fanning 14 Oakland A's on June 13.

29

Powerful outfielder Albert Belle.

The amazing Frank Thomas.

and the rest of the pitching staff faltered all year long. The team finished 80–81, and Bevington was fired. "It was a humbling experience for all of us," admitted Thomas. "I don't ever want to go through that again."

The Chicago club anticipated another banner year from Frank Thomas after his AL batting title (.347 average) the season before.

WHITE SOX REGROUP FOR THE FUTURE

After the team's dismal performance in 1997, the White Sox were determined to turn things around. "There's no reason we should struggle like we did," observed Albert Belle. "But now that's over, and we have to concentrate on getting better." If Chicago does improve, it will be on the strength of the team's power-packed lineup. Speedsters like second baseman Ray Durham and outfielder Mike Cameron look to set the table for big bangers Frank Thomas, Belle, and Robin Ventura to drive them in. "We'll have no trouble scoring runs," said general manager Ron Schueler. "We just need help with our pitching."

The White Sox will look for Navarro to rebound from an off year, and the team expects big things from young pitchers James Baldwin, Matt Karchner, and Jason Bere. "A lot has happened to us that would have destroyed other teams," explained Thomas. "But we're still together and we're going to make a championship happen here in Chicago." With two of the game's premier talents leading the way, it might not be long before Belle and the Big Hurt put a big smile on the faces of Chicago's South Side fans.

32

DATE DUE			
		Do	
		not	
		stamp	
		here	